SO-AHU-138

Alfred Noble Library
32901 Plymouth Road
Livonia, MI   48150-1793
(734) 421-6600

J567.913
N

Dinosaurs

Brachiosaurus

Livonia Public Library
ALFRED NOBLE BRANCH
32901 PLYMOUTH ROAD
Livonia, Michigan 48150-1793
(734)421-6600
LIVN #19

Daniel Nunn

Heinemann Library
Chicago, Illinois

$20.71   19 J

MAR 0 1 2008

© 2007 Heinemann Library
a division of Reed Elsevier Inc.
Chicago, Illinois

Customer Service 888-454-2279
Visit our website at www.heinemannraintree.com

All rights reserved. No part of this publication may be reproduced or transmitted in any form or by any means, electronic or mechanical, including photocopying, recording, taping, or any information storage and retrieval system, without permission in writing from the publisher.

Designed by Joanna Hinton-Malivoire
Printed and bound in China by South China Printing Co. Ltd.

11 10 09 08 07
10 9 8 7 6 5 4 3 2 1

The Library of Congress has cataloged the first edition of this book as follows:
Nunn, Daniel.
  Brachiosaurus / Daniel Nunn.
      p. cm. -- (Dinosaurs)
  Includes bibliographical references and index.
  ISBN-13: 978-1-4034-9449-8 (library binding - hardcover)
  ISBN-13: 978-1-4034-9456-6 (pbk.)
  1. Brachiosaurus--Juvenile literature. I. Title.
  QE862.S3N86 2007
  567.913--dc22
                          2006030056

Acknowledgements
The publishers would like to thank the following for permission to reproduce photographs: Alamy pp. 6, 10 and 23 (Mike Danton), 22 (www.white-windmill.co.uk); Corbis pp. 7 (Galen Rowell), 12 (Jim Zuckerman), 22 (Louie Psihoyos); Getty images pp. 18 (National Geographic/Maria Stenzel), 19 (Science Faction/Louie Psihoyos), 20 and 23 (The Image Bank/ Grant Faint), 21 (News/Cancan Chu).

Cover photograph of Brachiosaurus reproduced with permission of Corbis/Jim Zuckerman.

Every effort has been made to contact copyright holders of any material reproduced in this book. Any omissions will be rectified in subsequent printings if notice is given to the publishers.

3 9082 10802 7643

Contents

The Dinosaurs

Dinosaurs were reptiles.

Dinosaurs lived long ago.

Brachiosaurus was a dinosaur.
Brachiosaurus lived long ago.

Today there are no *Brachiosaurus*.

Brachiosaurus

Compsognathus

Some dinosaurs were small.

But *Brachiosaurus* was very big.

Brachiosaurus had long legs.

Brachiosaurus walked slowly.

Brachiosaurus had a very long neck.

Brachiosaurus could reach the top of trees.

Brachiosaurus ate plants.

Brachiosaurus ate stones, too!

Sometimes other dinosaurs
attacked *Brachiosaurus*.

Brachiosaurus used its feet to fight back.

How Do We Know?

Scientists have found fossils
of *Brachiosaurus*.

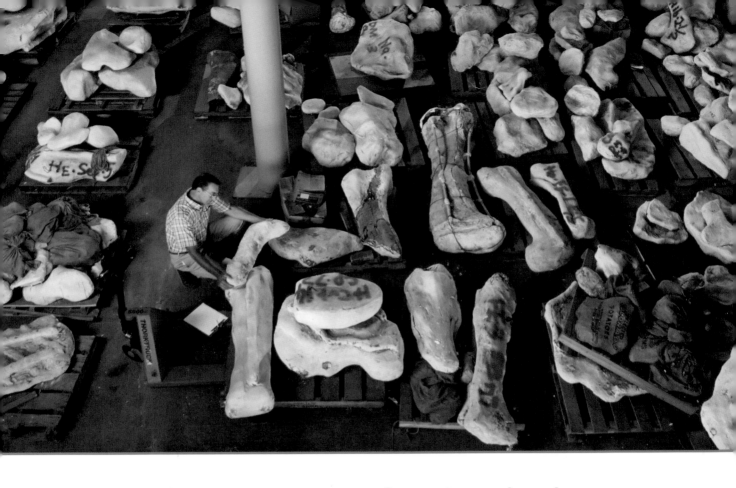

Fossils are parts of animals that lived long ago.

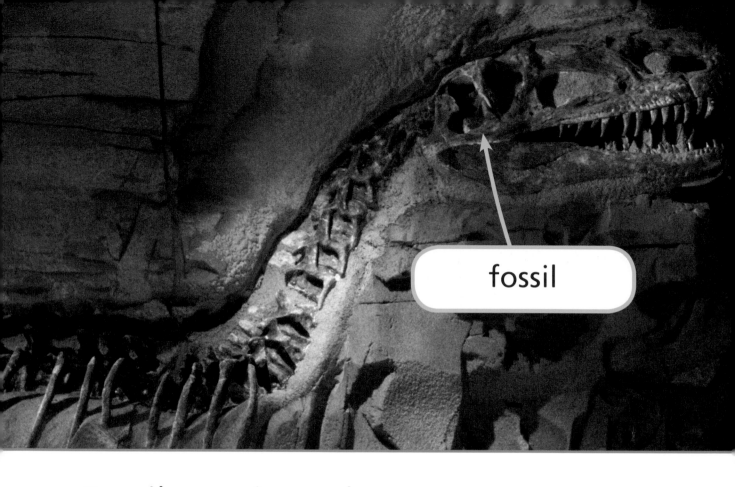

fossil

Fossils are in rocks.

Fossils tell us what
Brachiosaurus was like.

Fossil Quiz

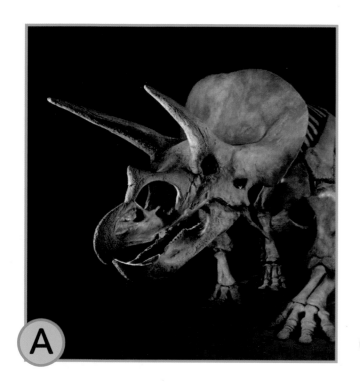

A

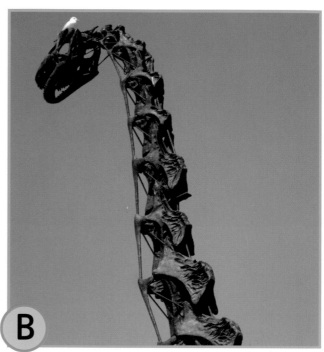

B

One of these fossils was *Brachiosaurus*.
Can you tell which one?

Picture Glossary

dinosaur an animal that lived long ago

fossil parts of a dead animal that lived long ago

reptile animal that is cold-blooded. Snakes, lizards, turtles, and alligators are reptiles.

Answer to question on page 22
Fossil B was *Brachiosaurus*. Fossil A was *Triceratops*.

Index

Notes to Parents and Teachers

This series gives a first introduction to dinosaurs. In simple language, each book explains the physical characteristics of different dinosaurs, their behavior, and how fossils have provided a key into our knowledge of dinosaurs' existence and extinction. An expert was consulted to provide both interesting and accurate content. The text has been carefully chosen with the advice of a literacy expert to ensure that beginners can read the text independently or with moderate support.

You can support children's nonfiction literacy skills by helping students use the table of contents, picture glossary, and index.